I LOVE YOU, MOUSE

JOHN GRAHAM

I LOVE YOU, MOUSE

Pictures by
Tomie de Paola

Harcourt Brace Jovanovich, Publishers
San Diego New York London

HBJ

Requests for permission to make copies of any part of the work should be mailed to: Permissions, Harcourt Brace Jovanovich, Publishers, Orlando, Florida 32887

Printed in the United States of America

Library of Congress Cataloging in Publication Data

Graham, John, 1926-
I love you, mouse.

SUMMARY: A child imagines the things he would do with various animals if he were one of them.
[1. Animals—Fiction] I. De Paola, Thomas Anthony. II. Title.
PZ7.G7526Iad [E] 76-8022

ISBN 0-15-332874-6 (Library: 10 different titles)
ISBN 0-15-332886-X (Single title, 4 copies)
ISBN 0-15-332946-7 (Replacement single copy)

For Sophia Jane, My Mouse

I love you, mouse,

and if I were a mouse,
I'd make you a furry nest.
And we'd curl up together
and nibble some cheese.

I love you, kitten,

and if I were a cat,
I'd make you a soft basket.
And we'd drink warm milk
and stretch ourselves.

I love you, puppy,

and if I were a dog,
I'd build you a kennel.
And we'd play tag
and, sometimes, chase a cat.

I love you, piglet,

and if I were a pig,
I'd build you a sty.
And we'd dig roots
and loaf in the mud.

I love you, chicky,

and if I were a chicken,
I'd build you a coop.
And we'd scratch for corn
and chase a butterfly.

I love you, lamb,

and if I were a sheep,
I'd build you a strong fold.
And we'd graze in the pasture
and grow wool for sweaters.

I love you, cub,

and if I were a bear,
I'd find you a cozy cave.
And we'd hunt for some honey
and watch out for bees.

I love you, tadpole,

and if I were a frog,
I'd find a quiet pond.
And we'd splash in the pond
and have races you'd win.

I love you, duckling,

and if I were a duck,
I'd find a blue lake.
And we'd swim all day long
and go "quack-quack."

I love you, gosling,

and if I were a goose,
I'd find a wide marsh.
And we'd play hide-and-seek among cattails
and go "honk-honk."

I love you, bunny,

and if I were a rabbit,
I'd find you a safe burrow.
And we'd play in the moonlight
and eat clover and carrots.

I love you, owlet,

and if I were an owl,
I'd find you a warm tree hole.
And we'd fly together, all night long,
and call out "who-who."

I love you, baby,

and since we're people,
I've built a house for you,
and given you a bed with warm quilts,
a cool drink of water,
a kiss on the nose,
and a quiet good-night.

0
C 1
D 2
E 3
F 4
G 5
H 6
I 7
J 8